JAN BRETT

HEDGIE'S SURPRISE

SCHOLASTIC INC. New York · Toronto · London · Auckland · Sydney · Mexico City · New Delhi · Hong Kong

ISBN 0-439-26037-X

Copyright © 2000 by Jan Brett. All rights reserved.
Published by Scholastic Inc., 555 Broadway, New York, NY 10012,
by arrangement with G.P. Putnam's Sons, an imprint of
Penguin Putnam Books for Young Readers, a division of
Penguin Putnam Inc.. SCHOLASTIC and associated logos
are trademarks and/or registered trademarks of Scholastic Inc.

20 19 18 17 16   4 5 6/0

Printed in the U.S.A.   08

First Scholastic printing, September 2001

Designed by Gunta Alexander. Text set in Palatino.

Once there was a speckled hen who laid an egg every day, only to have it taken by a little Tomten every morning. It all started because the Tomten got tired of porridge for breakfast.

Each morning the rooster crowed as the sun came up and Henny knew the Tomten was on his way. So did the little hedgehog who lived nearby.

The Tomten always called out to her, "Henny! Have you got a little yummy for my hungry, hungry tummy?"

The Tomten climbed into the hen house, took Henny's warm, smooth egg, and ran off to cook it in his little kettle, sprinkle it with salt, and gobble it down. Then he fell fast asleep in the hayloft until evening.

Henny didn't like the Tomten taking her eggs, but
she put up with it until one morning when she saw

Goosey-Goosey sail forth, smiling and bowing, with a stream of piping goslings following her.

"Oh, my," Henny clucked. "Where did all those little ones come from?"

"My eggs are hatching," crooned Goosey-Goosey. "Here comes the last one now."

From that moment on, Henny wanted a brood of peeping chicks of her own. But how could she stop the Tomten from taking her eggs?

The next morning when the Tomten poked his head in, Henny tried. She clucked loudly and pecked. She flew at him, but nothing stopped that hungry Tomten from taking her egg again.

"No eggs, no chicks, no peeping babies."

Henny wailed so loudly that she woke up the little hedgehog, her tears pouring down on top of him.

Puffa-puffa. Stick-stick, Hedgie went, as he crawled out to talk to her. "Poor Henny. I've been watching the Tomten take your eggs. I'll help you trick him into stopping."

The next morning when the rooster crowed, there was the Tomten. "Henny, have you got a little yummy for my nearly empty tummy?"

Henny and Hedgie were ready.

The Tomten reached for an egg and pulled out an acorn. "Hmmm," said the Tomten. "What's this?" And off he went to try it. The acorn was tasty, but it didn't fill him up and he awoke in the middle of the afternoon, grumpy.

The next time the Tomten arrived looking for an egg, he found a bright red strawberry. It looked bigger than the acorn so he ran off to cook it.

The strawberry was jammy and sweet, but it only filled up the Tomten a little more than the acorn had, and he woke up early.

The sun had just come up when the Tomten was at the
hen house again, his stomach roaring with hunger.

Pushing Henny aside, he grabbed for an egg, only to find
a delicious smelling mushroom. He raced off to cook it and
as scrumptious as it was, he woke up with his little tummy
growling for more.

"Cock a doodle . . . !" The Tomten rushed in even before the rooster finished crowing.

"Henny, have you got something for my hollow, hollow tummy?"

This time he found a smooth, round potato, even bigger than an egg. He cooked it quickly, swallowed it down, and went back to his hayloft.

He woke up at sunset only half full. The Tomten had had enough.

"Henny," he shouted, "tomorrow I want an egg for breakfast and nothing else. If I don't find one, I'll eat you up instead!"

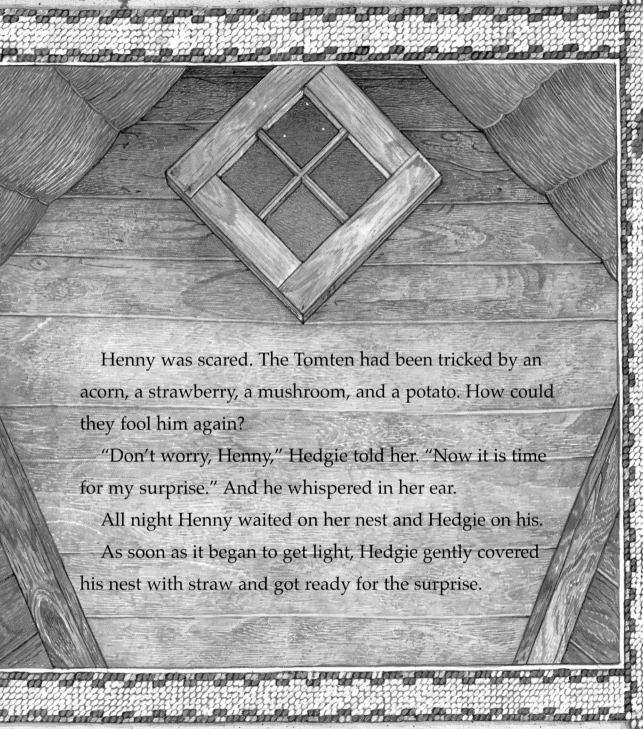

Henny was scared. The Tomten had been tricked by an acorn, a strawberry, a mushroom, and a potato. How could they fool him again?

"Don't worry, Henny," Hedgie told her. "Now it is time for my surprise." And he whispered in her ear.

All night Henny waited on her nest and Hedgie on his.

As soon as it began to get light, Hedgie gently covered his nest with straw and got ready for the surprise.

Henny and Hedgie could hear that Tomten's stomach rumbling like thunder a mile away. He burst into the hen house, pushed Henny aside and GRABBED.

"Ow!" he howled. "Ow, ow!"

Puffa-puffa, stick-stick! He had clutched Hedgie, all closed up in a tight round ball of needle-sharp prickles.

Henny and Hedgie listened as the Tomten ran home, yowling.

"Thank you, Hedgie!" Henny said, looking at her dear friend. "I'm sure that Tomten won't be back here again for breakfast. But what I can't figure out is, where have you hidden my eggs?"

Just then Henny heard a little peep, then another, coming from Hedgie's nest. She looked over and saw the straw begin to move. Five baby chicks peeked out of their shells and fluffed up their down. As Henny settled down with her babies nestled around her, the Tomten's mother was in the hayloft making breakfast for her hungry Tomten.

"Hedgie, Hedgie, Hedgie.
You are full of surprises," Henny cried
as she led her baby chicks out into the sunshine.

But the little Tomten didn't hear a word. He was sound
asleep, his tummy full of tasty porridge.